Cinderella's
(Not So) Ugly Sisters

For my mother,
with love and thanks.
– G.S.

To Lou-Caroline
(my little Californian cousin!)
– B.D.

First published 2014 by Macmillan Children's Books
a division of Macmillan Publishers Limited
20 New Wharf Road, London N1 9RR
Basingstoke and Oxford
Associated companies throughout the world
www.panmacmillan.com

ISBN: 978-1-4050-2161-6 (HB)
ISBN: 978-1-4050-2162-3 (PB)

Text copyright © Gillian Shields 2014
Illustrations copyright © Bérengère Delaporte 2014
Moral rights asserted.

2 4 6 8 9 7 5 3 1

A CIP catalogue for this book is available from the British Library.

Printed in China

Cinderella's
(Not So) Ugly Sisters

Written by
Gillian Shields

Illustrated by
Bérengère Delaporte

MACMILLAN CHILDREN'S BOOKS

Once upon a time, in a town far away, there were two sisters called Winifred and Prudence.

La-la-la!

They weren't exactly beautiful, but they were the nicest girls anyone could ever meet.

Their mother, Widow Fairpenny, gave piano lessons. She saved what little money she had in her best teapot, for emergencies. Though the family wasn't rich, Fairpenny Cottage was always full of music, laughter and love.

Every Saturday, Baron Spendit brought his beautiful daughter, Ella, for a piano lesson at Fairpenny Cottage. People felt sorry for Ella because she had no mother. Win and Pru thought that she was absolutely perfect.

"Isn't she lovely?" sighed Win, who was short and round.

"Like a dainty princess," said Pru, who was tall and lanky.

But although Ella seemed lovely on the outside, she was horrid on the inside.

Her nanny was a Fairy Bad-Mother who gave her anything she wanted.

Yet Ella still demanded more!

Win and Pru didn't know that of course, and they
were utterly delighted when Ella and the Baron
began to call every day. The Baron always smiled
and bowed and kissed the Widow's hand.

So it was no surprise when, a few weeks
later, he asked the Widow to marry him.

"How wonderful!" exclaimed Win.

"Ella will be our sister!" cried Pru.

The wedding day soon arrived and it was absolutely splendid.

Win and Pru played sweet music on the horn and violin,

and Ella looked like the perfect bridesmaid in a fancy new frock.

All the townsfolk cheered and joined in the celebrations. It was the happiest day of Win and Pru's lives!

But the very next morning at Fairpenny Cottage,

their poor mother found a broken teapot . . .

and a note.

"What about me?" cried Ella when
she heard the news about her father.
"We'll look after you," said Win.
"We're sisters now!" added Pru.

"Sisters! You're far too *ugly*
to be my sisters!" screeched Ella.
"My father only married your
mother for her pot of money!"

And she flounced off and locked herself in the kitchen.

Ella ordered her Fairy Bad-Mother
to tell everyone that her step-sisters
had locked her away and treated
her like a servant.

"That will stop people droning
on about how nice they are!"
she said spitefully.

The Fairy Bad-Mother's spell worked, and the town gossips were outraged to hear that Ella had to do all the work at Fairpenny Cottage.

"Those sisters make her scrub the floors!" they fussed. "And clean the cinders from the fireplaces!" they fumed.

"Poor little Cinder-Ella!" the townsfolk fretted.

It wasn't long before people stopped coming for piano lessons, so the family had no money and nothing to eat.

But in the kitchen, Ella had plum pudding and strawberry tarts, all by magic.

And if that wasn't enough, she made the Fairy Bad-Mother hurtle nasty spells at poor Win and Pru through the keyhole.

Purple spots appeared on Win's nose, and Pru grew enormous ears. "We really are ugly now," they sighed.

The Three Sisters
Fairpenny Cottage
Fairpenny Lane
Fairytale Kingdom

A few days later, three magnificent
invitations arrived from the palace.
"We've been invited to Prince Smarming's
ball," cried Win excitedly.
"Please come with us, Ella!"

Ella opened the kitchen door and grabbed her invitation.
"I'm not going to the ball with my UGLY SISTERS!" she sneered.
And she slammed the door in their faces.

On the day of the ball Ella ordered the
Fairy Bad-Mother to magic her a new dress.
"And get me a decent carriage!"
she snarled.

"Temper, temper!" cackled the fairy.
"Now remember the magic will only last
until midnight," she warned, as she waved
Ella off in her dazzling new coach.

Meanwhile, Win and Pru arrived at the ball and were very excited to see Prince Smarming.

But he just tittered at them.

"I'd heard you were plain," he sneered, "but not *ugly!*"

"Isn't Smarming horrid?" said Win.

"Just awful!" replied Pru. But she was far more interested in the orchestra.

"Doesn't that violinist sound wonderful?"

Moments later, Ella made a sensational entrance.

He was hooked, like a silly fish. And he wouldn't dance with anyone else all night.

"What a girl!" Prince Smarming goggled, as he shimmied over to dance with her.

Just before midnight,
Ella pulled off her slipper
and wrote her address on it.

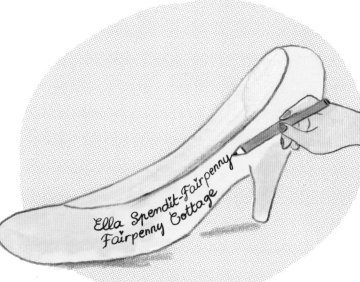

Ella Spendit-Fairpenny
Fairpenny Cottage

"Come and find me tomorrow,
Smarmy," she whispered.
As the clock struck twelve,
she ran away, leaving the
slipper behind her.

The next day, Prince Smarming headed
straight to Fairpenny Cottage,

where he found his Cinder-Ella
and asked her to marry him.

Everyone flocked to see the royal wedding. They thought

Prince Smarming and Cinder-Ella would live happily ever after.

But it wasn't long until . . .

she ran off with the Duke of Dollar.

Dear Smarmy,

I am tired of being married to you. The Duke of Dollar has offered me all the ~~money~~ love in the world.

So I am off.

Your unloving wife,

Ella

Win and Pru didn't miss Ella. The Fairy Bad-Mother's spells soon began to fade and they turned back to their nice ordinary selves.

Pru married the violinist from the palace orchestra and Win married the man with the big bass drum.

The whole family lived together at Fairpenny Cottage, and their lives were always full of music, laughter and love.

Which shows that you can have a fairytale ending, even if nasty people call you nasty names!

But as for Ella . . .

She was still cross,

and mean,

and dissatisfied.

And that made her look

really quite . . .

UGLY!